PEANUT GOES FOR THE GOLD

Pursue the things that bring you joy, not because of where you want to end up, but because of the happiness that they bring you right now. Even if other people don't understand your rhythmic gymnastics journey, the only person who really needs to understand it is you. —JVN

For Liza, for giving me my little peanut. —GR

ISBN 978-0-06-294100-8

The artist used Adobe Photoshop to create the digital illustrations for this book.

Typography by Chelsea C. Donaldson

20 21 22 23 24 PC 10 9 8 7 6 5 4 3 2 1

First Edition

PEANUT
GOES FOR THE GOLD

JONATHAN VAN NESS

pictures by Gillian Reid

HARPER
An Imprint of HarperCollinsPublishers

Peanut has their own way of doing things.

Peanut loves doing **cartwheels**

while on the basketball court

and having **banana pancakes**

on their birthday instead of cake . . .

. . . and cutting their own hair as they **Hula-Hoop**.

Sometimes people think Peanut's weird . . .

. . . but more often, friends wind up joining in the fun.

When Peanut decides to do something, there's
just no stopping them.
"I'm going to be a **rhythmic gymnast!**"

"And here's what my routine is going to look like!"

"Dad, I need you to help with my **outfit**."

"Mom, I need you to help with my **choreography**."

"And Sammy, man, you need to pick out my **music**—and make it funky!"

Peanut practiced their routine night . . .

. . . and day.

Peanut practiced at **home**.

They practiced at **school**.

They practiced **on the bus** from home *to* school.

SCHOOL BUS

And when the day for the big competition came,
Peanut was sure the routine was perfect.

The music was all cued up,

and Peanut **danced**

and **spun**

and **tumbled**

and **dove**.

They **swung** the hoop

and **tossed** the ball

and **juggled** the batons . . .

. . . and **twirled** the ribbon.

Peanut's performance was flawless . . . almost.

Peanut only forgot one thing . . .

. . . to tie their shoes.

But instead of ruining the act, Peanut turned that stumble into a **triple-axel tumble!**

And they totally **stuck the landing**.

Peanut knew it was the perfect routine . . .

… and the judges couldn't help but agree.

Yep, Peanut just has their own way of doing things—

even if they're still learning how to tie their shoes.